Also by Salvatore Ala

Clay of the Maker
Mosaic Press, 1998

STRAIGHT RAZOR AND OTHER POEMS

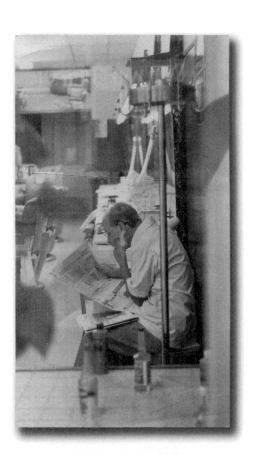

Straight Razor
and Other Poems

Salvatore Ala

BIBLIOASIS

LIBRARY AND ARCHIVES CANADA
CATALOGUING IN PUBLICATION

Ala, Salvatore, 1959–
Straight razor and other poems

FIRST EDITION

Poems
ISBN 0-9735971-3-5 (LIMITED ED, CASED)
ISBN 0-9735881-0-1 (PBK.)
I. Title.
PS8551.L3S77 2004   C811'.54   C2004-905366-3

PRINTED AND BOUND IN CANADA

For my wife Brigitte
and my children
Michael and Josephine.

CONTENTS

In the hall of pain, what abundance on the table.
The music endures, but not the music-maker...
Czeslaw Milosz (1911-2004)
from "A Mirrored Gallery"

The Nightstand

At twenty I had a job, car, and apartment,
Paid vacations, and opportunities for advancement.
Everything I needed, but for a nightstand,
A place to set alarm clock and lamp.

At a used furniture store I bought a nightstand,
And inside the drawer there was a book.
Not the Gideon Bible of hotel rooms,
But *The Complete Poems of Keats and Shelley.*

What is fate but the opening of a magic box,
The turning of pages and a night without sleep.
As I read, I became the things I read,
And by morning I was transformed.

Homage to Pablo Neruda

Proprietor of a travelling bazaar
Of potent elixirs strained from jungles,
Vials in which rivers rage, flasks of cloud,
The granite voices of Macchu Picchu;
And impure things: wheel ruts, blood and semen,
The severed heads of dictators,
Letters from kings, propaganda;
An earthflow of love poems; and elemental things:
Lemons, artichokes, melons, and salt;
Also magic potions, locks of hair,
Moonlight fossilized in stone, emeralds
From the mines of Columbia; snakeskins,
Ports of call, arrivals, departures...
Lastly, Chile, like a child's model,
Raised by the whale spine of the Andes,
With its copper-colored people,
Their stone flute music of mountain mist,
Their poverty, and their dignity...
Your human cry of the human market.

The Chinese Masters

How great are the ancient Chinese poets.
They are masters of what they do not say.
They walk on rice paper and leave no step,
And move silently through the green bamboo.

When you read the poem of a Chinese master,
You feel as though some Shaolin priest
Has snatched a pebble from your hand.
How much you have yet to learn.

The House of Poe
Baltimore, MD

In the garret of that two-storey house on Amity street
(Now a slum within a ghetto within the projects
of America), Poe transmigrated his soul
From poetry to the palace of fiction,
Paying with poverty for the rich coins of his metre.
How could his penniless nerve survive sobriety,
With a paralytic grandmother, his brother
    Coughing up blood,
A debtor's prison, and love haunted by death.
Eureka! Poe would return to Baltimore
To write the last cryptic page of his life
In the book of despondency and madness.
When the door of literary fame opened
He saw the ghouls and hags inside.

Poetry Prize

I've been awarded a prize for my poetry.
What is it?
Oblivion.
Congratulations.
Thank you.

We who make art in solitude,
Make solitude richer by art.

Notre-Dame-des-Neiges Cemetery
Montreal

Though I walk amid myriad gravestones,
The summer air is soft, trees cast full shadows,
And the grass ripples from grave to grave.
When a cloud passes, the shadows deepen.
I see Emile Nelligan, sixteen years old,
Brooding because he has fallen in love
With poetry and beauty. A breeze blows through him.
I think of Albert Lozeau, the invalid poet,
And the cold window of his solitary room;
And of the sleepless young Sylvain Garneau
Gazing at the sky from his own grave;
And of how lucky I am to be thirty-two,
Hearing the voices in the summer winds.
Ah, la belle vie, la belle vie… the dead are saying.

In Memory of Czeslaw Milosz *(1911-2004)*

Reading you
After hearing of your death,
Again my eyes are bathed in poetry's water,
Raindrops anoint me with clarity,
Every poem is a living garden,
My eyes are touched by words.

Once again through you
The clear and deep language
Of poetry speaks to me,
And tells me it is still possible
To live with one another,
Free of the violence
Of a life without poetry.

You who have died,
Now you are inside your poems,
Breathing life
In that earthly paradise you created,
That on the day of your death,
Your life should be as everlasting.

On a Portrait of George Rodenbach *(1855-1898)*
   by Levy-Dhurmer

So sensitive was the poet,
He was like a drop of rain
In which a city is reflected.

The Cancer Library
for Alden Nowlan 1933-1983

If we could find a cancer grammar,
Precancerous prose, language toxins,
White blood cells in poetry,
We could create a cancer library.

This way to the heart's archives.
Quiet while the reader softly weeps.
O we might even find a cure,
If only we were sensitive readers.

A Belated Eulogy
for Joseph Cote (1931-1994)

If anyone could recognize a poet
When he heard one, it was Joseph Cote.
Among his many gifts he had a poet's ear.
While hometown barflies, blowhards, and poseurs
Saw him as just another drunkard,
I knew Joseph Cote as a man of letters,
A traveller, collector of fine art, and a generous friend;
No one ever looked better in a crumpled suit.
When he cried for wilder music and stronger wine,
It was only that he might clear his head,
And for the muse to come singing
Some lines of verse that were infused in him.

Pathetic Fallacy

The most noxious landfill is language.
Books are polluted; libraries, dump sites.
Due to toxic levels of pathetic fallacy
Bookstores have been closed by the Board of Health.
All reading, boycotted by Greenpeace.
Why must a cloud be forever *lonely?*
Why must the sea be always *cruel?*
Our books are fairytales for grownups,
With magical forests of *sad* birds, *evil* snakes,
Happy flowers, and *gloomy* trees,
Where we sit in the *melancholy* shade,
Ourselves the center of the universe,
And seldom consider the rivers of refuse,
Created by culture's industrial waste.

City after Rain
Washington, D.C.

After the intense Atlantic squall,
Runnels and rivulets stream down buildings
As though down mountain-sides.
The very bricks wash acid smooth
And mortar crumbles from every gap.
Pillars drift in the rain and become many.
The soaking rains soften cement,
Water pools over granite
And steel begins to bend.

After the rain, green lichens grow bright
On the wet black bark of trees.
Every green is now greener.
Streets are wide rivers of reflected light.
The earth rises and the city is less real.

After the rain, marble is sticking to wet leaves,
Walls are dripping from ivy,
Monuments and memorials
Cling lightly to the air.

Motor City Rap

Driving west down Jefferson East
Between the mansions of Grosse Pointe, Michigan,
And Lake St. Clair—past the house of Edsel Ford,
Toward the antique wealth of Indian Village.
On this hot muggy Saturday night,
The mayflies have risen from the lake bed.
Living clouds swarm the streetlights
And drift like smoke amid the trees.
Then Jefferson Avenue molts its affluence.
We enter the night of another city. Burned out cars
Parked outside abandoned buildings.
A black cop shaking down a black youth
In a liquor store parking lot. A crowd happens.
The heavy traffic stalls on mayfly wings.
Rap is blasting from every car.
When crackheads look up to the sky
Stars are scattered rocks of crack cocaine.
Upon the mansions of Grosse Pointe
The mayflies amass, leaving their stain.

City of Cats
Palermo, Sicily

In a city of cats shrill voices pierce rooms,
Clusters of jungle grow in parking lots,
Thick vines hang down from balconies,
Botanical gardens creep out of fences,
And alleyways become rutting grounds.
More than the all-night caterwauling,
All the terrifying and orgiastic voices,
Rabid loners with bared fangs drooling,
One senses the crumbling city being overrun.
On nights like this the city vanishes,
Felis libyca stirs, shadows stalk the ruins,
Nothing left but wild cats, and the rising sea.

And you beside me sleeping, fitful,
Night speaking through your dreams.
Manic laughter stilled to a purring breath,
Then the night cries of sexual shadows,
Then the fear again, ailurophobia,
Clawing the sheets as I stroke your hair,
And scratch your shoulders and back.
She whom I knew, where is she now?
The body of a sphinx lies across the night.
I know her by the feral smile on your face,
And I who have been listening am afraid,
Afraid to sleep or to dream or to wake.

Florence, 1993

It was the night after the car bombing of the Uffizi.
The city was a vandalized painting of itself.
I walked the via Inferno, to via Purgatorio,
And saw a prostitute on a street corner
Pointing the way to paradise. I saw
A collapsed bridge in a burning river.
Every sculpture was writhing with animal pain,
Every tomb thrown open, every masterpiece blackened.

My shadow led me like a spirit-guide
Amid the howls of lamentation;
The street was a river of boiling blood.
Then I saw a light and a passageway.
Above the doors of an old church I read:
Lascaite ogne speranza, voi ch'intrate.*

---

* *Give up all hope, you who enter here.*

Christmas Prayer for the Millennium
December 5, 1999

To you, God of all gods,
Whether you are real or not,
I offer up this heartfelt prayer
For the end and the beginning:
Bring down every church,
Lift every trace of your word
Like dust from every page,
Transform your cross and altar
Back into tree and rock,
And fade even your remoteness
From human memory:
Restore every believer to the silent clay
Of your miraculous earth,
That we might remake ourselves,
And enter the new millennium
As murderers and profiteers,
Not the hypocrites of our atrocities.
Amen.

Leda and the Swans

When the woman felt herself penetrated,
She was for a moment breathless at being so deeply filled,
The long neck lying between her breasts,
The god rushing hotly into her out of swan.
Such is the myth of transformation and seduction.
Our ancestors too must have had inhibitions,
To have created a bestiary of desire.
When I was eighteen I saw a porn flick
That showed a woman being mounted
From behind by a German shepherd
Until the image blurred into absurdity.
Centaurs, mermaids, satyrs, and sirens,
Farm boys and sheep, a stripper and her python…
How is it we are so ashamed of one another,
That we demonize the animals with our repression?

The Octopus

I found myself on some desolate shore.
A tree was growing there I had never seen,
With large leaves and purple flowers.
When waves crashed without a sound
I began to sense that everything was unreal.
Hidden by the leaves, in the broad crown,
I saw a giant octopus.

O cephalopod, you who walk on your head,
And vanish in clouds of ink,
My mollusc brain convulses.
I see your Paleozoic ancestors crawling
Out of the ocean and walking on land.
I see human beings with eight legs,
With the bodies of octopi and squid.
What skilled artists we would be,
Painting from within the color of our skin,
Glowing in the deep sea-dark night.
What genii with oceanic intelligence,
Flattening our bodies to squeeze through cracks,
Knowing the language of dolphins and whales.

Restless through the night the sea carried me.
Without a soul I was not afraid.
Before the vision faded the dream was over.
I awoke in my own bed and rose on two legs.

The Silver Maple

As they cut down our tall and spreading Silver Maple,
I stand outside to watch the old tree die.
For eighty human years it put forth leaves,
And was the crown and shade of this backyard.
One of the tree cutters said that a felled tree
Gives off its essence all around you.
As branches fall a sapling grove springs up,
The light turns green, air so pungent
With the living wood inside the bark,
I breathe another kind of air and feel more alive.
And though the old tree is almost down
When I look up it's still above the pines,
Ragged canopy of fluttering silver leaves,
Before darkness covers my tree of light.

Déjà vu

I know a clearing between the pines
Above the lake.
My shadow flies off the cliff.
I remain standing.

Visions of a Country Road

On each side of the country road
Lean tall old trees far into their shadows,
And you feel a desire to turn off
Into the landscape of yourself,
To the end of a road that never ends…
And all that solitude yours.

Go deeper, to where fence posts end,
Beyond the rusted out car
Now stranded in vines,
Where farm land becomes meadow and woodlot,
And the meadowlark is a clear song
Of space and light.

There the footings of a house
Fill in with wild grass and flower,
Like a house built by the rain,
And shining through itself
A wild barn becomes a holy place.

The deep rustling of the trees
And swaying shadows on the road
Call us from our destination
To a landscape beyond the highways,
And the nowhere of being lost.

Land Snails

I sensed the forest path was moving,
As though water was flowing under my feet,
Carrying pebbles, leaves, and twigs along
And making the smallest trickling sound.

When I looked down at the path
I saw hundreds of land snails afoot,
Crawling as snails do at a snail's pace,
But a mollusc migration after a night of rain.

I had never seen so many snails,
Like stones creeping along the path,
And time slower than I knew time could ever flow,
Carried me upon the shells of snails.

Fossil Record

So faint the imprint of this fossil leaf
It seems the thousand year old shadow
Of a falling leaf.

Peyote

On peyote you cross the Devil's Highway
To the mystical oasis of Quito Baquito,
Where the roots of cottonwood, mistletoe, and tule
Tug at the springs of the chemical desert.

Before the colors of night blaze like the colors of day,
You hear the drums of the sun's rising—
The spirit voices in the desert winds
The desert winds in the spirit voices.

Your senses are the things they perceive.
Like a desert you are everything around you.
In the arid spaces of saguaro, mesquite,
    and the Joshua tree
You are pierced by the plumed arrow of peyote.

Living Mask

The American Indian woman,
A hundred and six years old,
Had a face vivid with ancestral lines,
Like a clay mask baked in the sun
And dried by the winds of open spaces.
She wore the spirit mask of the earth.
She never died, the songs say,
The rains washed her away.

The Searcher

Are you searching for something, anything?
I know a man who travelled the world,
Who studied history and philosophy,
Who failed at a life of art and crime,
Who stupefied his will with many drugs,
Then became a boring-again Christian.
After two years of sinful deprivation
He suffered an overdose of salvation,
And admitted himself to a hospital
With visions of angels and demons.
Though he is fifty, he looks seventy.
I sometimes see him by the river,
Where he practices Tai Chi and meditates.
The river is forever flowing, forever still.

The Window

Does anyone stand at a window tonight?
Is there another person in all the world
Who grows transparent,
As the night and the stars
Pass into him?

Island Light
for Renato Guttuso

Although it is night
And the sea storms
Against the cliffs,
Lemon orchards light the coast.
In the green night of the leaves,
A lunar darkness glows.

A Riddle at Mondello

At that seaside resort on the Tyrrhenian Sea
The night dissolved me into the all,
Sifted me into fine grains of sand,
My shadow passed into moonlight.
Suddenly, I was a face, a glance,
A hand closing on other hands.
Who was I among history's multitudes?
I left no footprint by the sea.

A Child's Symphony
  for Josephine

Children are the musicians of play.
Rosy-cheeked horns, blue-eyed flutes, little blonde bells,
Plump drums of their mothers' hearts.
Loud is their only volume.
Cacophony is their Mozart.

Whatever squeaks, squeals, whistles,
Drums, taps, smacks, pops, toots,
Dings, whirrs, chimes, peals, ticks,
Jingles, clinks, patters, clacks,
Blows, buzzes, quacks, trills,
Cackles, twitters, hums, or sings…

Will bring the children with their little chairs,
Their instruments of sweet discord,
Their maestro of pure sound
Who bangs the big wood spoon on a pot,
And calls all to attention
On the stage of endless play.

Family Tragedies
in memory of Salvatore Ala

My dear *mongoloid* cousin and namesake,
Wallet-maker, scholar of bus routes,
Box scores, and table etiquette,
Handling your Al Kaline autographed baseball
With the delicacy of a jeweller.
Who could have loved you more
Than your loving mother and sister,
Fulfilling your days with admiration
For your slightest accomplishment.
When they were struck by a car
And killed crossing the road,
At the funeral you and your father were inconsolable
With the idiot pain of being no one.
After he died you were institutionalized
Among the deranged, the demented,
Until you were no longer human.

He Claps His Hands...
for Frankie

He claps his hands above his head,
Makes Indian whooping calls,
Then with his finger strums his lips.
He spins a pot lid like a spinning top,
Flicks the light switch on and off,
And likes picture books of airplanes,
The photographs of *National Geographic*.
He can mimic a dog, a cat, and an owl...
His smile is all crooked teeth and eyes.
When he claps his hands above his head,
We clap our hands above our heads.
When he makes whooping calls, we call back.
When he strums his lips, we strum ours.

The Heaven of Handicapped Children

Where space flows like water,
So that nothing is hard or sharp,
Everywhere the pliant, buoyant, firm,
Infinitesimal balance of motion,
Equilibrium's endless flowing
From every direction holding, releasing…

Or eternal and simultaneous interchange
Of subatomic and celestial particles,
Infinite number and regression,
The farthest point always near.
Gravity's first rising.

Or regeneration's genesis,
Beginning of all emerging,
The birth before birth.
Genealogy's first molecule,
Progeny's spring and curative.

Or clarity's deepest water,
Simplicity's essence distilled,
The weightlessness of all need
Where love is greater than chaos.

A Father Speaks to His Children

The old Europeans are dying,
Their cemetery is the twentieth century.
They were baptized by the blood of their time,
Those immigrants of back-breaking labor.

Pour concrete with your will.
Lay bricks with your mind.
May the only assembly line you ever know
Be the days that build your future.

Money is the gnashing teeth of the world.
Politics is the banker who absconds
With the wealth of his lies.
Seek your self among the lost.

Religion is a murderer
On the streets of history.
Use faith to make you human
And fantasy to make you divine.

Straight Razor

Watching my father shave a face
I saw how he held the straight razor
At an ever-changing angle
As his hand worked along the jawline,
Around the mouth, beside the ear,
Over the throat, the artery…
As though carving a face
Out of wax, with no waste.

Barbers

for my father, uncles, and cousins

The child I was sits trembling in a barber chair.
Make me a barber, I asked my father,
Barbers are men who smell like rose oil,
Who gather sea foam in their hands.
In my family, scissors fly like swallows,
Straight razors never bleed.

Now mirrors have tears in their eyes,
Combs and brushes are buried in coffins.
My father is inside a mirror,
Walking in his white salon shirt,
Carrying his sad combs and scissors
Along an endless seashore.

Haircut and Shave

When a man in a hospital bed
Needs a haircut and shave,
The barber with his black bag
Goes humbly through the wards.

In shadow and in light,
The barber and his patient,
Seen through an open door.
A smile on the sick man's face.

The Barber has No Place to Cry

Cutting hair at the rest home,
My father was afraid of growing old.
The old have so few hairs
And to shave a lonely face can break your heart:
You never shave the same face twice.
Alone and sick, sickness a blessing,
There were some old people, my father said,
No one ever visited, only the barber.

Tools of the Trade

Sometimes I need a comb
To comb the tangled hairs of many lines,
And barber shears to trim a poem
Like a beard that suits my face.

Sometimes I need a straight razor
To shave a poem of day-old stubble,
And sometimes I need a brush,
My brush of form and thought.

Thank You, Poetry

Thank you, poetry, for my father's barbershop,
For the barber chairs and soap machines,
For the windows and mirrors, for it being downtown,
For the movie theatre and marquee next door,
For opening nights and the Saturday matinee.
Thank you for the barbershop magazine rack,
For the hours I had to read and wait,
Mirrors sinking my thoughts into dreams.
Thank you, poetry, for the weight of scissors,
For the fragrances of Clubman hair products,
For the sounds of the razor on the strop,
For the razor on the back of the neck,
For the hot towels and sting of aftershave.
Thank you for the bus rides downtown,
For my mother helping my father close,
So we could all go home together.
Thank you, poetry, for the magic
Of those mirrors, for the poetry hidden there,
For letting this quiet boy, the son of a barber,
Experience something of your presence
Among such humble things.

Sweeping the Barbershop Floor
for my brothers

They never forget they are brooms,
Barbers' sons grown into men.
The advantage of being a broom:
It teaches you a broom's humility.

At the end of a day when you sweep
The last of the hair away,
You do not feel inferior to those whose hair
You take out in the trash.

A Childhood Pharmacopoeia

Bay leaf and parsley twined my infant caduceus.
I was fortified by egg whites spiked with vermouth.
In our cellar hung bunches of roots
    and drying plants.
Grape leaves on my forehead drew out the fever.
A sea glass of salt water washed my sore throat away.
Olive oil poured rustling trees into my aching ear.
And chamomile tea was like some mythic meadow
On a summer morning in eternity.

Magic potions in the house of childhood,
Mason jars serving as apothecary jars
Still sealed in cellars that no longer exist,
I am going back to the sickbed of childhood,
Where my mother treats me with medicines
    made by her hands,
Where my father stands over me and I live forever.

Dago Red
for my brothers

Brothers, it makes no difference
If we use *Zinfandel, Barbera,* or *Sangiovese...*
We change our blood into wine.
Even if we wash our grapes
Under the harvest moon,
Sulfur smouldering in the night;
Even if we ferment our wine
In a Hiram Walker's whiskey barrel
To make a headier vintage, a deeper bouquet,
We change our wine into blood.
Ourselves we pour into cups.
Ourselves we taste.

Unloading Watermelons at the Windsor Market

It took two men and three boys
All day to unload four thousand jumbo watermelons
Off two eighteen-wheelers that had just come up
From a watermelon patch in Georgia.
By the end of the day they were so heavy
You couldn't feel your hands,
But we dropped thirty out of that many.

For the first time I was working with men.
The men sang Sicilian folk songs
As they heaved into the load of melons,
And I worked to the rhythm of their rough voices.

Nothing quite so red and wet and cool
As a cracked open watermelon on a summer day,
So hard and green a shell
To hold that much water and light.
Hot on the outside from the growing days in the fields
To the heat of this day in our hands,
Their cool waters quenched our thirst.
They were both our bread and drink.

What sweet pollens of sunset
Summer spreads upon the wind;
Flowers from which swell this immense fruit,
Red honey in a hive of black bees.

On the bus home my body slept.
My fingers were smooth as the fine sand
On the rinds of melons.
All night I was like a vine and my head was growing.

Grandmother

Quieter than the quietest of quiet things,
My grandmother was a whisper.
We shared a bedroom for five years
When *nonno* died and I was a boy.

Quieter than the quietest of quiet things.
A hand smoothing out a sheet, a breath,
Is yet too loud for how she woke
While I was sleeping, then never woke again.

My Mother's Bread

When I eat my mother's bread
I taste my mother's breast.
My mouth fills with strong milk.
I am an infant again.

What I can't remember
Is still in my flesh.
Kitchen heat, the odor of yeast,
White dough rising, flour on her face,
Breasts swollen with milk,
The warm bread of her hands
On my face and lips.
Sleep coming over me.

My Life in Opera

Growing up in a house of pain,
You sacrifice everything for love.
Like the time my uncle tore open his shirt
And begged his brothers
To let him return to the love
He left in Buenos Aires.
Like the time my mother
Was scratching at her eyes.
Like the time my father both raged and wept.

Days were scenes without direction.
One day a cousin would stab herself
Or an aunt jump from a tower.
I didn't know what was real.
But what passionate singing I heard,
Tenors, sopranos, baritones,
All around me in full voice;
And there I was, in love with *Tosca*,
Condemned to death,
And just twelve years old.

Madame Butterfly
for Rose Mary

In my version of Madame Butterfly
There is no heartbreak and suicide.
Through panel-rooms the sound of the ocean.
On a silk screen, the blue moonlight.
One gust of wind and it is Spring.
Butterfly wings flutter on bronze,
The temple bells are ringing,
Flower and song flow into one.
No tear drop moistens a sleeve.
No dagger falls to the floor.
No shadow-feast is served.
Riding a dragon across the ocean,
Cio-cio-san's husband returns alone.
All night the nightingale floor is singing.

A Summing Up

My childhood was a sea voyage,
A barbershop and the ringing of a mandolin.
Summer stars through grape leaves,
Prickly pears and fig trees,
Snails creeping out of straw baskets,
Silence and violence.

My childhood was a stuffed baby alligator
That swims in the swamp of memory.
Twice-haunted identical twin sisters
Who survived a plane crash.
Playing cards scattered on a table,
Voices shovelling graves.

My childhood was a broken accordion,
A winepress pressing me.
Chinese faces at the market,
Hunting rifles behind glass,
Dried eel at the fish store,
Rain of motherless time.

The Guitar Player
  for Giuseppe Principato (1926-1980)

Strange how after so many years
I can still hear you playing your guitar.
The strings ring out in my memory
Like circles widening in water.

No matter how many card table arguments,
How many fists pounding tables,
How many funeral prayers
And wedding bands I heard growing up…

Beyond it all I hear you strumming
Your guitar on summer afternoons;
And how for a time even our loudest relatives
Would bend their ears to listen.

The Accordion of Orlando Bracci *(1919-1960)*

You have to use body and soul to work an accordion
   The way Orlando Bracci played:
Sweet as wine, sharp as a diamond,
     Harmonious as a summer wind,
   A coil winding tighter and faster.
They say when Orlando Bracci played *Spanish Eyes*
   The music would possess him.
Women put down their cards, men stopped fighting,
   As he swung his hip into the accordion,
His arms crushing the music inside his chest,
   And pulling it out again.
Playing as though he wanted to tear the accordion apart
   And save his own life,
Through all the music that was in him.

The Uncanny

The composition by Koshkin
On *The Fall of the House of Usher,*
Was tonight the most haunting music
The guitarist performed;
Though it wasn't the wild ringing of dissonant chords,
But the blue flash of lightning
At the window of the recital hall,
Which for a second
Made the guitarist look like a dead man
Picking a bone guitar.

The Cellist

When she plays,
Were I the Stradivarius
Between her thighs,
So that when she bows
The strings of my being,
I could give back
What she is giving me.

Composition in Gray

November, you are the urn of the seasons,
All other months are ash inside you
Body without light, spirit-haunted.
Our waking hours
Resemble more a rainy dream,
Our dreaming, the mist of another life.

I hear an oboe in November,
A lone oboe piercing through the woods.
An oboe in black,
Accompanied by strings.
Are not those cellos and violins
Our desires dying even as they desire more life?

From the river a freighter's foghorn
Throbs in the night.
The rumbling of a distant train
Beats drum rolls for the dead of November.
I dream them in gray.

Along the river's mist I see the dead,
And then I see her
Who once was naked beside me.
How ashen her beautiful face.
How dead those eyes I knew.
She holds out a cold hand.
I step through to the other side.

Love in the Catacombs
Palermo, Sicily

Though we go solemnly
Through the catacombs,
Alone with you among the dead
I sense the swelling of my sex,
I become engorged in the catacombs
And feel the hardness of death.

Before our time becomes time
We should make love so many times,
Our bodies create a lasting wave
On the ocean of physical time.

Let us leave this monk's cave,
Climb out of this pit of bones,
Come back from the underworld
And cross the ancient river,
Forgetting darkness and silence,
The dry odorless air,
For the blazing light
And congestion of traffic,
For our bed and room
With its wide windows on the blue sea.

In the catacombs
I touch your hand.
My shadow turns to stone.

Nautical

When we make love,
I am the mast
And you are the sail.
I am the bowsprit
And you are the night.

Woman as Wave

When you sleep your body is a wave
Washing in from the gulf of Mexico…
All the waves that have ever washed over us.
Wave of the ankle and the calf,
Wave of your thigh and hip,
Wave of your waist and of your breasts,
The waves of your arms and shoulders,
And the waves of your hair.
Near you on the restless sea of our bed
I feel the waves of your breath
And the waves of your dreams,
And I know you are a crashing wave,
A wave that dies within a wave,
A wave upon the sea of night.
You are the first born of all waves,
The wave at the meeting of waters,
And the deep waves of feeling that never rise.
Wave of my love for all of time,
Like a line of poetry that is the wave
Of the body on the sea of its shadow.

The Study of Languages

My love is like the crescent moons of Arab calligraphy,
The swords and sand waves of the desert.

She is also like the little word houses of China,
Shining on their bamboo stilts
As the green rice flashes to the east.

Sanskrit is the mystic knowledge of her eyes.
Again and again the wall servants
Of the Pharaohs lead me to her in silence.

If I spoke Aramaic I could tell you
Of the myrrh and frankincense of her flesh.

Latin is the mirror of her beauty.
Ancient Greek is our Olympus,
Our long climb to the mythical sublime.

Spanish is for the blood rose of her mouth,
French for the azure of her eyes,
Russian for her madness and passion.

She is like the inscription on a stone,
More obscure as it is revealed.

At the Museum of Natural History
  Washington, D.C.

We are bone, love, we are earth.
Our breathing slows and we are stone.

We are flesh, love, we are spirit.
Our eyes close and we are mineral.

We are burial places, love, we are fire.
When we kiss the ice ages recede.

We are fossils, love, missing links.
When we touch the earth grows fecund.

They will find us, love, on a seashore
Buried in each other for ten thousand years.

Last Will and Testament
for Brigitte

To my wife I bequeath the gold of my being,
The erect memory of night, my hands on her face,
My body upon her body, my eternal kiss,
The memory of my eyes behind her eyes.
To her, my books of precious metal,
My library of ashes, my silent music,
My photographs without a body or a place,
The masterpieces I never painted,
The bonds of my desire and affection,
The rare coins of my coldness and indifference,
My shadow in the sunlight of the infinite.
To my wife I leave the poems I never wrote,
For them to whisper only to her, to say
My fortune was poetry, my poverty is death.

Acknowledgements

I want to thank Daniel Wells and Dennis Priebe for their hard work; Professor Walter Skakoon, for his excellent critical readings and advice; and also my dear friend Len Gasparini for our many celebrations of poetry. Thank you also to Edyta Stachowicz for her photographic expertise. And my most heartfelt thanks go out to Beata Stachowicz, who makes my days possible; and especially my wife Brigitte, who makes my nights and days possible.

Some of these poems first appeared in broadsides. "Barbers" and "The Barber has No Place to Cry," were published in the *Windsor Review*.

Salvatore Ala was born in Windsor, Ontario in 1959. He studied philosophy and literature, and has worked at various jobs. His first book, *Clay of the Maker*, was published by Mosaic Press in 1998. He has also published five broadsides of his work. His poems have appeared in numerous journals; and most recently, in the anthology *Sweet Lemons, Writings with a Sicilian Accent*, Legas, 2004. Salvatore lives in Windsor with his wife and children.

Straight Razor and Other Poems was designed and typeset by
Dennis Priebe. Set in Adobe Garamond and Optima it was
printed on Zephyr Antique Laid in an edition of 500 softbound
and 15 hardcover copies by Gaspereau Press in Kentville, Nova
Scotia. The hardcover edition was hand bound by Daniel Wells
using hand-marbled papers made by Lucy Lapierre.

BIBLIOASIS

WINDSOR, ONTARIO, CANADA